Father, We Thank You

This Book
Was Donated By

RUBY & ELLERY COLEMAN

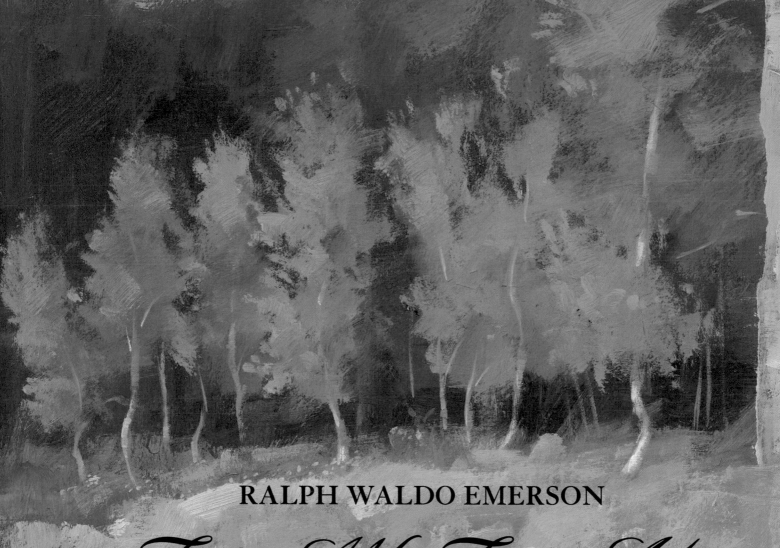

RALPH WALDO EMERSON

Father, We Thank You

Illustrated by

MARK GRAHAM

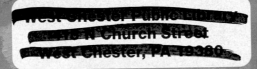
SeaStar Books ❧ NEW YORK

For flowers that bloom about our feet,
Father, we thank You.

For tender grass so fresh and sweet,
Father, we thank You.

For song of bird and hum of bee,

For all things fair we hear or see,
Father in heaven, we thank You.

For blue of stream and blue of sky,
Father, we thank You.

For pleasant shade of branches high,
Father, we thank You.

For fragrant air and cooling breeze,

For beauty of the blooming trees,
   Father in heaven, we thank You.

For rest and shelter of the night,
Father, we thank You.

For this new morning with its light,
Father, we thank You.

For *health and food, for love and friends,*

For everything Your goodness sends,

Father in heaven, we thank You.

ABOUT THE AUTHOR

Ralph Waldo Emerson was born in 1803 in Boston, Massachusetts. He entered Harvard Divinity School at the age of twenty-one, and became a minister like his father and many of his ancestors. After serving as rector of Boston's Second (Unitarian) Church for about three years, Emerson gave up this ministry and became a popular lecturer in the Boston area.

Emerson is widely considered one of the most important thinkers of nineteenth-century America, and was one of the country's first environmental advocates. His work greatly influenced many writers, including Henry David Thoreau, the author of *Walden*. Emerson died in 1882, in Concord, Massachusetts, at the age of seventy-eight.

To Mom and Dad
—*M. G.*

Illustrations copyright © 2001 by Mark Graham
Book concept and biographical sketch copyright © 2001 by Alan Benjamin

SEASTAR BOOKS
A division of NORTH-SOUTH BOOKS INC.

First published in the United States by SeaStar Books, New York, a division of North-South Books Inc., New York.
Published simultaneously in Australia, New Zealand, and Canada by North-South Books,
a division of Nord-Süd Verlag AG, Gossau Zürich, Switzerland. Library of Congress Cataloging-in-Publication Data is available.

The art for this book was prepared using oil on paper.
The text for this book is set in 28-point Granjon Italic.

ISBN 1-58717-072-8 (trade binding)
1 3 5 7 9 TB 10 8 6 4 2
ISBN 1-58717-073-6 (library binding)
1 3 5 7 9 LB 10 8 6 4 2

Printed by Proost NV in Belgium

For more information about our books, and the authors and artists who create them, visit our web site: www.northsouth.com